Elizabeth Willoughby Varian

Never Forsake the Ship

And other Poems

Elizabeth Willoughby Varian

Never Forsake the Ship
And other Poems

ISBN/EAN: 9783337397661

Printed in Europe, USA, Canada, Australia, Japan

Cover: Foto ©Andreas Hilbeck / pixelio.de

More available books at **www.hansebooks.com**

NEVER FORSAKE THE SHIP,

AND OTHER POEMS:

BY

"F I N O L A."

DUBLIN:

PUBLISHED BY MAC GLASHEN AND GILL, SACKVILLE STREET,

1874.

TO

THE PEOPLE OF IRELAND,

OF ALL CREEDS AND CLASSES,

THIS VOLUME

IS AFFECTIONATELY DEDICATED

BY

FINOLA.

" And oh, it were a gallant deed
  To show before mankind,
How every race, and every creed
  Might be by love combined—
Might be combined, yet not forget
  The fountain whence they rose,
As filled by many a rivulet
  The stately Shannon flows."—

THOMAS DAVIS.

PREFACE.

THE impassioned poems of "FINOLA" are not the frothy ravings of a spasmodic heart, weary of home-life, panting for stage effect ; nor yet the diseased perturbations of a nervous system, in tightened bodice, and hot-house air. They are the outpourings of a heart akin to nature—reared in her solitudes, beside her basaltic columns, her shamrock lawns, and her arbutus groves. The "Silk of the Kine" has lowed to that heart, and, with appealing eye, won it to high resolve. The crumbling seat of learning on every lovely isle, and glorious headland, have evoked the reverence of that heart; the embattled walls—its courage and calm defiance. Its democracy it has learned from Christianity—to level upward its sacred aim. To sound a trump of Hope, a harp of Rapture, would be, in a well-ordered state, its loved employ ; but, looking from its cradle-bed on an unrecognized nation, and a famine-stricken people; on a rotting roof-tree, and glassless window; on a "bar-brigade," and a homeless people—the trump of Hope breaks into a blast of horror or defiance, and the rapture of the harp into a piteous appeal for organization, attention, and instruction. Much better would it have accorded with such a heart to have intoned a message of love and peace to all men, but when clean hands lift up the silver cornet of the Lord, 'tis not for mercenary hire : 'tis then the thunder of offended Justice that peals in the impassioned strains of its servant, and the tears of Heaven's own heart that wail in the murmurs of its swelling lyre.

The Irish ready wit, the harmless banter, the wild joke, the irrepressible fun, are not unknown to that heart ; but with the pen and the lyre she moves only as Heaven inspires, whose voice, in this, would seem to say—Erin shall not now be the laughter-mover of the world : she has a sworn duty to fulfil. "REMEMBER ME !" Yes ! dear shadow of our land, we will remember thee ! As it behoves children of a great parent, in-heritors of a brilliant fame, aspirers after an unrotten state—where the barren wastes shall blossom, and the very trees upon the hill-side clap their hands for joy !

And now, having said so much, introducing " FINOLA "—if she, to any Irish heart, need an introduction—I retire ; assured in my very heart that this, her first legacy to Erin, will be fruitful of emotion, hope, and faith—the best wealth which can be showered upon the head of any state.

RALPH VARIAN.

BRIDAL MORN ANNIVERSARY,

Thursday, 27th May, 1874.

CONTENTS.

Little you reck of the warring strife,
The passionate conflict that knows no rest,
Yearning to succour a Land oppressed.

" Be there a thousand—I am one ; or, if our strength
Have but one hundred left,—Sylla is braved by me ;
If only ten continue—I will be the tenth ;
And, if but ONE remain—I, THEN, THAT ONE WILL BE."

VICTOR HUGO.

NEVER FORSAKE THE SHIP.

Never forsake the ship!
The keel drives on through the heavy sea,
Like a plough-share cleaving the furrowed lea,
Tossing aloft bright wreaths of spray—
Feathery buds of the ocean's May;
Coronals white as the stainless snow,
Shine in the wake of the vessel's prow:
Oh! never were blossoms so pure and fair
As the vapoury jewels glistening there.

Never desert the ship!
The land lies yonder through cloud and foam—
Ever steer on for our distant home:
Though the tightened cordage snap in twain,
And the creaking timbers shiver and strain;

B

Though the sluggish sails may droop and fall,
Like the heavy folds of a funeral pall—
The breeze will awaken, the wind uprise,
And the brave barque speed under sunny skies.

Never forsake the ship !
Hope may wither and courage fail,
If faith sustains us no need to quail ;
Oh, blinded vision—oh, darkened sight,
Pierce through the gloom of the shrouding night :
Though the longed-for haven be hid from view,
Believe that a home awaiteth you :
Mariners ! pause not to idly deplore
The rugged path to that promised shore.

Never give up the ship !
By the sunken rocks and the shelving strand
Guide her still on with a firm brave hand,
Steering away for the chainless sea,
Her sails all set and her flag flung free—
So let us wrestle for freedom or life
Where the hurricane wages a generous strife,
No hidden reef, like a treacherous foe,
Lying in ambush to strike a blow.

Never desert the ship !
Even though perils be brooding near,
Turn not aside with the recreant's fear ;

No one can tell when the heavens may lower,
And the fierce storm burst in its terrible power,
And the lash of the sea, like a slave-driver's whip,
Fall with its wrath on the beautiful ship.—
Set her to rights, men, and keep her afloat,
Nor slink in your dread to the life-saving boat.

Never forsake the ship !
The mast may be shattered, the white sails be rent,
And the tapering spars, like a reed, may be bent ;
Yet, cling to the barque, though her timbers may yawn,
And the rudder you steered by be parted and gone,
The fast-holding anchor be wrenched from the chain,
And her beams from the stem to the stern rent in twain :
Flinch not, brave comrades, but terror dispel,
Though her strong oaken ribs be crushed in like a shell.

Never desert the ship !
Heed not the crash that has sundered the deck,
Remember your oaths, men, and stand by the wreck ;
The keel's lying upmost, the mainmast below,
And the sea-weeds dank tangles are wreathed round
      the prow—
Gird up your souls, there is glory in death !
Who would not strive for the martyr's pale wreath ?
With brow still undaunted, and firmly set lip,
Let a wild cheer ring out, and go down with the ship !

Rosaleen.

Rosaleen listened, struck dumb with scorn :
    Only a flash of the downcast eye,
Only the gust of a stifled sigh,
A tremulous flutter of pulsing heart,
A clench of the hand and a sudden start—
    Told how the blow was borne.

    Listened in silence—too proud for speech :
Fast fell the torrent of arrogant hate,
The senseless clamour of tongues irate,
Questioning, doubting that cherished faith
Kept, like a gem, without spot or scaith—
    Daring HER truth to impeach !

    Turning aside from the buffeting word —
No answering taunt her lips essayed,
Though the pallid brow wore a deeper shade,
When stung by their cruel ribald cant—
She shrank, like the leaves of the "sensitive plant"
    By careless fingers stirred.

Bravely she held in her grasp the rein,
Though the swelling throat and the brimming eye,
And the pale lip struggled for mastery :
Standing erect in her stately pride,
Entrenched by the foes she so oft defied—
　By her glance was falsehood slain !

Many had sought to defile her name
(For Rosaleen strayed from the narrow groove
Where circumspect custom must ever move) :
Little they dreamed of the quenchless power
Hid in the heart of the folded flower—
　Of each deathless hope and aim.

Wounded by slander, by wrath deep stung,
The smouldering embers of passionate ire
Flashed and quivered with sudden fire ;
Wan was the lamp, as a lily's cup,
Till the light of the prisoned flame leaped up,
　Like a burning cloven tongue.

Woe to the power that had lit the ray,
That kindled the flash of the lightning eye,
And aroused the spirit of mutiny :
Noting each stroke of the throbbing heart,
The firm-clenched hand, and the fitful start,
　They quailed in their mute dismay.

Like the silvery peal of a clarion's note
The words rang out, soft, clear, and low,
Yet deep as the sound of a torrent's flow :
Oft had they heard that voice before,
But the altered tone her accents wore
　　With remorse the slanderers smote.

" Guilty or not ? let the world decide—
For screening the lamb, untimely shorn,
And tending the bird from its warm nest torn ;
For shielding the fragile drooping flower
From the heavy charge of the thunder shower—
　　I am ready to be tried !

" Dare you asperse my maiden fame
Because that I differ from lying wrong,
And side with the weak, and repulse the strong ?
Though I may fail to avert the blow,
Pitying love can I still bestow,
　　Heedless of praise or blame.

" Little you reck of the warring strife,
The passionate conflict that knows no rest,
Yearning to succour a land oppressed—
Is it not womanly, holy, and pure ?
Dearer the faith that you bid me abjure
　　Than the perilous gift of life !"

Rosaleen paused—for the storm was o'er :
Fronting the foe, with a dauntless eye,
She stood in her conqu'ring majesty ;
Pale was the lamp, as a cup of snow,
The fierce flame ebbed, and the fitful glow
Kindled and flashed no more.

Coming Home from Mass.

Coming home from Mass !   What thoughts those
    simple words call forth,
As here I sit the live-long day, beside my cottage
    hearth ;
The treasured gems from memory's mine, like gold
    sands in the stream,
Through the warm current of my tears, but brighter.
    fairer seem :
I see no ruin on the green—the chapel still stands
    there,
The village chimes are ringing through the clear and
    frosty air ;

And mark yon group of peasant girls—God bless
　　them—as they pass ;
No fairer sight could meet your gaze—they're coming
　　home from Mass !

The autumn leaves that fall around are faded, seared,
　　and dead,
Unlike the flowers on mem'ry's waste, whose bloom
　　has never fled ;
The very embers on my hearth with burning radiance
　　glow,
Their kindly glances seem to light the forms loved
　　long ago ;
The streamlet through the feathery fern speeds, singing
　　on its way,
Amid the foam-girt islets—fitting homes for sprite and
　　fay.
I used to think ('twas childhood's dream) how happy
　　I should be
As queen of one sweet fairy isle, unconquered, proud,
　　and free !

I longed to share the wild bird's sway, whose moss-
　　built palace stood,
Like a citadel of feudal chief, above the mimic flood ;
To gather from the rainbow sward the sweetest flowers
　　that grow,

And twine them in a matchless wreath to crown my
childish brow.

But dearer fancies soon were mine: I still a queen
would reign—

My heritage, one leal brave heart, I loved, nor loved
in vain,

The tell-tale blush, the stolen kiss, the whispered word
—alas!

That happy time is gone when we came, hand in hand,
from Mass.

Old scenes again come thronging back, as billows 'fore
the storm,

Casting, like sea-weed on the strand, some dear re-
membered form,

A ringlet from a fair young brow, a bright eye flashing
free—

These are the rescued relics flung from mem'ry's fearful
sea.

Once more I lead the village dance—sought, loved,
caressed by all;

The shamrock scarcely bends its stalk beneath my
light foot-fall.

But, hush! a whisper in my ear :—" The moments
swiftly pass,

Your promise, Norah, don't forget when coming home
from Mass!"

I see the *soggarth's* kindly smile, I hear the blessing
  given,
Which shone around my daily path, a beacon-light to
  Heaven ;
He takes my trembling hand in his : the blush on
  cheek and brow
Reveals the secret of my heart—disguise were idle
  now.
For me no ruin haunts the green, no pastor's grave is
  there,
The pealing of the village chimes, in fancy, still I
  hear ;
Fresh flowers are strewn before my steps, all cheering
  as I pass,
Upon the bridal morn, when we were coming home
  from Mass !

THE SHIP WILL SAIL TO-MORROW.

THE ship will sail to-morrow : all is o'er—
  The struggling hope, prolonged from day to day,
Died like a summer sunset : never more
  Shall joy for us arise with golden ray.
The last sad hour draws near—oh, God, the *last !*
Would that the midnight of despair were past.

Parted for ever! mournful dirge be still;
  Hushed be the heart's wild wailing—'tis in vain
To combat fate with firm and stubborn will,
  Or seek from shattered chords to strike one strain.
Stem the hot rain of tears, be mute the cry
Wrung from the spirit's depths of agony.

The world looks coldly on : it cannot guage
  The measure of our anguish : what were words—
Brief, weak, and trite—our sufferings to assuage,
  To blunt the grief piercing like two-edged swords?
The eye may scan the surface—can it know
Aught of the storm that rages far below?

The ship will sail to-morrow : skies are fair,
  Fresh is the breeze, set westward towards the sea;
The surplus of our race the land can spare :
  Thin out the rank growth—sapling, shoot, and tree;
Weed from the o'er-stocked garden, leaf and root,
And trample down the refuse under foot.

It matters not the quivering fibres bleed—
  Life's current ebbs, who cares to staunch the wound?
Passing upon the other side, none heed
  The victim's cry, by pain and suffering bound.
Oh, earnest truth!—the heart alone can feel
The bitter pang that words can ne'er reveal.

To-morrow! and the numbered hours steal on :
 I scarce can speak for these fast-falling tears :
I thought the tumult of despair was gone,
 For what have *I* to do with hopes or fears ?
A lonely waif, tossed on the desert shore,
The storms of life can buffet me no more.

Is all prepared ? take down the linnet's cage,
 And twine around the bars fresh dewy leaves,
The feathery fern, and sprigs of thyme and sage
 And trailing woodbine from the cottage eaves.
Poor Mary's bird ! her dying gift to me ;
I'll tend it day and night upon the sea.

Have you forgotten (I must whisper low)
 The green sod from our mother's holy grave ?
Never o'er us shall Ireland's daisies grow—
 Our resting-place may be beneath the wave.
There wrap it up, my heart grows faint with pain,
I must not look upon THAT sight again !

Here is the rose tree from our garden plot,
 The pallid primrose from the shady brake,
The violet, and the blue forget-me-not,   .
 And our own shamrock, loved for Ireland's sake :
Another soil must nourish leaf and stem,
The skies of home can never shine for them.

Oh, that these weary eyes might but behold
   The far-off glimmer of the coming morn ;
And the dark future for this heart unfold
   The fate that to our country shall be born :
My grateful song of joy should never cease—
" Lord, let thy servant now depart in peace."

The ship will sail to-morrow ! all is o'er :
   The hope, prolonged from torturing day to day,
Died like a summer sunset : never more
   Shall joy for us arise with golden ray.
The last sad hour draws near—oh, God, the LAST !
Soon shall the midnight of despair be past.

To the Author of " Innisfail."

Meet offering for the bard—a nation's love,
   A nation's tribute nobly sought and won,
Oh, poet-laureate of our island home,
We thank thee : not with hollow word and speech,
Nor studied phrase, nor courtly eloquence.
The throbbing heart that leaps to hear thy strain,
The quickened pulse, the quivering tearful eye.
Proclaim a people's silent gratitude.   .
We knew not, recked not, of the buried wealth
That lay around. The river glided on
Singing the mournful burden of its song :

Unseen the glistening sands of burnished gold ;
The mine's dark bosom, rich in shining ore,
Retained its hidden splendour.   Not for us
Our country's buried glory : not for us
The countless stars upon her midnight sky !
From the wrecked argosy one loving hand
Gleaned the neglected spoil : the parted wave
Was bravely cleft ; the surge of time gave forth
The garnered wealth of ages.
Oh, fearless diver ! winning nobly back
From the dark waste of years that priceless gem,
A nation's heritage—her spotless fame !
Ah, little did we reck that 'neath the spray,
The blinding mist, the storm-rent billow's crest,
So fair a pearl was hid.   We little recked,
Until thy hand unveiled our country's sky,
That many a star, undimmed, was burning still.
Oh, dearly prized in winter's joyless hours,
The glowing flowers of June !   With loving toil
The wreath was twined : we noted but the thorns
Till thou revealedst the roses to our view.
AUBREY DE VERE ! far better than rare gem,
Or gleaming pearl, or golden-freighted stream
(That softly glides in whispered cadence by),
Or priceless ore, or summer's glowing flowers—
The gift for which thy country thanks thee well !

The Perfected Blossom.

THE pendant flower-stem bent beneath its freight
 Of fragile blossoms—delicate and white
The waxen petals, swathed in softest green—
Of equal beauty, each fair bud revealed
The promise of rich growth : no tainting blight
Stained the pure petals breaking into bloom.
It seemed a ruthless act to strip the spray,
A graceless deed to rob the snowy group
Of all, save one frail blossom—light and warmth,
The genial sunshine of a cloudless sky,
Ripened to radiant loveliness that gem.
So from this heart all lesser loves I tear—
One shall attain full stature, rounded, pure,
A perfect growth nurtured beneath the warmth
Of sunny glances : fervent melting rays
Shall woo the blossom till it burst in bloom.
My flower ! the priceless jewel of true love,
Oh place it in thy heart as in a shrine :
No cankering blight shall taint the snowy leaves
Stirred by the breath of passion—bear it still,
A deathless trophy, earth's most perfect gift,
THE LOVE THAT KNOWS NO SHADOW OF DECAY!

CHRISTMAS EVE AT SEA.

I HAVE no home to-night : the glimmering morn
    Will fling its lustre o'er the fierce wild sea ;
Dark is the sky, darker this heart forlorn.
    The Christmas dawn can bring no joy for me—
Nought save unspoken agony and grief,
And burning tears that fail to give relief.

Alone, aye, all alone, I pace the deck,
    Listening the music of the beating wave,
Far thundering o'er the desolated track,
    The storm's glad pæan, jubilant and brave ;
Louder the billow's song, the surge's sweep,
The grand old Christmas carol of the deep.

I have no friends, nor home—oh, bitter plaint,
    The crushed heart's eerie-cry— shall God forsake
The sorrow-stricken exile, sad and faint ?
    Can the wave's chime no answering echo wake ?
Hark to the tidings ! spirit, though forlorn,
Rejoice, for unto us a Child is born.

Poor doubting heart, the self-same midnight sky
 That spread o'er Judah's hills is lit for thee ;
The blessèd star, hung like a lamp on high,
 Flings its white radiance o'er the devious sea :
Shall it not guide the lamb back to the fold,
That light that cheered the holy men of old ?

I lift mine eyes, despite these blinding tears,
 And o'er the cold blank waters gaze in vain ;
Not even love can see through long dead years
 The "holy candle" shining from the pane—
Dead *years!* and yet unchanged the ivy's sheen
That decks the village chapel on the green !

Still the wild ocean anthem falls and swells,
 Stifling the sounds fast throbbing through my brain,
The blythesome carol of the merry bells
 For the lost exile ne'er to chime again.
Wrestling with anguish, what can it avail,
A spent breeze cannot fill the lagging sail.

Another league from land : vain baseless toil
 Counting the weary distance o'er and o'er,
Forging fresh links of misery, to coil
 Around a heart where hope can dream no more.
Hath the broad earth no home to-night for me,—
Woe for this Christmas eve upon the sea !

Speak Gently of the Dead.

Speak gently! one resentful word may cause remorse
    for years—
A heartless act, a thoughtless speech, can bring but
    bitter tears;
'Tis better far to shun the past, than seek, with impious
    aim,
To raise the darker side to view, with all its guilt and
    shame.
The moon's fair face is oft times veiled from our deep
    searching gaze,
We only note the gloomy pall that shrouds her gentle
    rays;
And thus, with ruthless will, we scan each cloud that
    meets our view,
A kinder glance will soon discern the brightness shin-
    ing through.

Oh! mockery of the true heart's wealth, to prize each
    cherished token,
With every show of lingering love, whilst cruel words
    are spoken;

To touch with gentle hand each gift, yet feign a deep
    regret
For fancied wrongs a generous mind would struggle to
    forget :
Perhaps a boon of little worth, a gem, or broken
    flower,
May bring the sad remembrance back of many a
    vanished hour ;
Oh, whilst ye mourn, with softened grief, the countless
    treasures fled,
And wear the gem, and bind the flower, speak gently
    of the dead !

Ye who have basked beneath the rays of fortune's
    dazzling light,
Can scarce discern the feeble gleams that cheer the
    sufferer's night :
The diamond wears a pallid hue within the hidden
    mine,
The sunbeams call the brightness forth that seemed
    too faint to shine.
And thus, adversity may dim those spirits born of
    Heaven,
But ye should mercifully judge, to whom so much is
    given :

They may have wandered from the path, by want and
    misery led—
Affliction hath a blighting power—speak gently of the
    dead !

It may be that ye have endured a studied slight or
    wrong,
Forgive, forget—doth just revenge to such as you
    belong ?
The slanderous tongue is mute, the hand that smote
    is pulseless now ;
Speak gently, for the grave-damp stains the pale and
    lifeless brow.
But, if the past *will* bring again each cruel word and
    look,
With all the countless injuries, so hard for man to
    brook,
The fierce retort, the scornful jest at which true hearts
    have bled—
Then, chiefly *then*, remember to speak gently of the
    dead !

LORD BYRON.

"The true story of Lord Byron's life."—Mrs. BEECHER STOWE.

FORBEAR ! nor drag the stagnant pool, the dark
    deposit of the past,
Not beldame's charm, nor witches' spell, the buried
    record forth may cast;
Accursèd foot that dares profane the hallowed grave
    with wanton tread,
To snatch the cerement from the corpse, and steal a
    march upon the dead !

Oh, worthless and ignoble deed, selling the very soul
    for gold,
And hollow fame now sunk to scorn—who heeds the
    tale by treachery told—
The dire detraction, baseless lie, the traffic of the false
    and mean,
The sordid infamy that seeks to pander to a taste
    obscene.

The startled nations, stunned and pale, are waiting
    still with listening breath,
But soon avenging tongues shall speak, and many a
    sword leap from its sheath—

Of what avail thy pigmy shield the onslaught of con-
　　tempt to spurn,
Each shaft that leaves the bended bow to thy cold
　　bosom shall return.

Oh, burning shame ! the loathsome asp to spue on
　　him its venomed slime,
To stain the lofty pedestal that stood unsullied through
　　all time ;
Where is the love that doubteth not, the charity that
　　thinks no ill,
The generous plea for one who strove man's noblest
　　being to fulfil ?

Aye, drag once more the sleeping pool—the world
　　looks on with eager eyes :
Bring all to light—the fair and foul from dense oblivion
　　must arise ;
Call forth each hidden grief, disclose the anguished
　　sorrow nobly borne,
The generous tears for others' woes—for dastard slaves
　　the abject scorn !

The records of a life too brief—each high resolve and
　　gentle deed,
The yearning impulse that impelled to aid the suffering
　　in their need ;

One land—ah, wherefore is she mute?—one land shall
    speak with words of dread :
Greece shall defend her patriot's fame, and stand
    between you and the dead !

UNDER THE BRIDGE.

THE midnight chimes rang out : the startled air
    Was freighted with the peals from spire and tower,
Till the spent echoes died within their lair.
    Softly the dew slept in each folded flower,
The wild bird brooded on her summer nest,
And worn sad eyes were closed in blissful rest.

Darkly the river surged upon its way,
    Turbid and rank and grim—a venomed snake
Gliding with stealthy tread—the foul murk spray
    Flecking with slime each object in its wake.
Like charnel lights, the lamps' dull glare came back,
Reflected from the waters' loathsome track.

O'er many a fair young head the stream swept on,
  Mid golden locks the ghastly tangles wreathed;
The conflict o'er, the weary guerdon won—
  By hidden graves the waters foamed and seethed,
Rich laden argosies sailed to and fro,
Unheeded slept the buried wrecks below!

Darkly the waters flowed with sullen swoop
  Through the blank arches, hurrying feet o'er head,
And grating wheels the ponderous fabric shook;
  Beneath reigned silence, drear and dumb and dead.
An ebbless tide, like some ill-omened bird,
Swept mid the darkness, though no sound was heard.

I said the darkling river poured its flood
  Through the dim arches—one was bare and dry,
A ghastly grotto by the wave withstood,
  A dismal vault black as the blinded sky:
Gaunt, spectral, shorn of even the pale lamp's glare,
And yet the pulse of life was throbbing there!

A pallid child stretched on the naked stones,
  Begrimmed and fouled—the bleeding blistered feet
Shivered with pain, and low half-sobbing moans
  Broke from the dreamer in his strange retreat.
Poor blossom! sin and blight with baleful power
Robbed of his heritage the human flower.

Mid misty hills, deep glens, the river rose,
   Pure, sweet, and chill, reflecting from the stream
The golden sunset at the day's soft close,
   The fern's green plumage, and the Mayflower's gleam;
Catching no fouler blot, no darker stain,
Than the cloud's shadow, and the falling rain.

Unsullied fount from whence the waters sprung,
   Pure source that gave the blighted spirit life;
If foul corruption and drear misery clung
   To the two wanderers tainted in earth's strife—
Both from their birthplace come forth undefiled,
The cold dank river and GOD's stricken child!

A cry rings forth—is there not one to save,
   To cleanse the tarnished jewel in GOD's crown?
It matters not the blind insensate wave,
   With its unburied dead, still hurries on.
Oh, for a helping hand to aid the wreck,
A beacon-light to win the lost waif back!

Laborare est Orare.

Mocking Heaven with supplications, chanted ritual, muttered prayer,
Offering feeble invocations, contrite tears of mute
despair—
Call you this the spirit's worship, and a homage meet
and true,
This the noblest, holiest duty, God and man require
of you?

What avail your jubilates, plaintive sigh, and fond
appeal,
Deep and fervent aspirations, and the rapt enthusiast's
zeal?
Can they raise your abject brother, can they rive the
bonds in twain,
Rend the hated shroud of error, and that brother's
rights regain?

Deem not that no purpose calls you, that no mission
waits for you:
Up men! diligently seeking what your hands shall
find to do—

Strive to bear the lamp of knowledge where earth's
  outcasts darkly dwell,
From the scared and blinded vision every gathering
  cloud dispel.

When the shattered wreck drifts past you—human
  waif so tempest tost—
Think, oh think, what priceless jewels may have been
  for ever lost,
Floating, drifting wildly onwards, mid the rock and
  stormy wave—
Oh, remember GOD will judge you if no hand is stretched
  to save !

Laborare est orare ! struggling ever for the right,
Bearing one another's burthens, pressing nearer to the
  light—
This a worship unrestricted by the forms of class or
  creed,
This a doctrine, pure and simple, that the feeblest
  mind can read.

Loving toil and earnest labour consecrate our common
  shrine ;
Pass not by, thy brother fainteth, freely pour the oil
  and wine—

This the mission that awaits you, this the work you
    have to do :
Laborare est orare, to that mission still be true.

Zealous thought, and stern endeavour—these our wea-
    pons keen and bright,
From the bended bow the arrow speedeth on its
    wingless flight ;
Not one word shall fall unheeded, from each seed
    some fruit must spring ;
Send thy message, no one knoweth where the dove
    may fold her wing.

Art thou not thy brother's keeper? toil brave heart,
    strong, willing hand ;
Raise that loved yet erring brother, free that brow
    from slavery's brand :
Fold the palms when labour endeth, sing the hymn
    when victory's won ;
Offer up your jubilates, when the glorious work is
    done !

UNA'S JEWELS.

PROUDLY she sat in her regal state, 'neath the quaint
    old hawthorn tree,
Blythe as the bird that sang o'erhead, happy, and wild,
    and free ;
An elfin queen on a mossy throne, mid a wealth of
    fairest flowers
That her tiny hand had gathered from the rifled wood-
    land bowers.

The rippling waves of light and shade through the
    shifting branches rolled,
Till the clustering curls of chestnut brown in the sun-
    beams turned to gold ;
And never on pictured saint reposed a brighter, holier
    glow
Than the radiance of the halo that entwined that baby
    brow !

A snow-shower from the weird old tree :—with a burst
    of childish mirth
She watched the hawthorn blossoms fall in silence to
    the earth—

The breeze, that softly rose and fell, sang a merry
roundelay,
And she deemed the spoil of scattered flowers a freight
of silvery spray !

The violet stars that decked her brow, and the down-
cast violet eye,
Seemed kindred jewels, darkly blue as the cloudless
summer sky ;
And the warm rich hue on cheek and lip shone bright
as a flashing gem,
Or the coral-tinted petals of the wild rose diadem.

A daisy perling on her breast, a daisy chain, and zone,
And a chatelaine of fox-glove bells that a fairy queen
might own—
She had piled a gilded barricade of May flowers from
the stream,
Nor wandering fay, nor charmèd sprite, could mar her
blissful dream.

Oh, priceless wealth, a heart to love the common things
of earth,
To find in the wild flower's folded cup a prize of rarest
worth ;

A Father's hand hath scattered wide true love-gifts for
    us all—
Alas, they coldly turn aside for whom those blessings
    fall.

How passing rich that infant heart, her wealth she
    deemed untold,
The yellow blossoms on the broom seemed stars of
    burning gold ;
The daisied mead was strewn with pearls, no casket
    could disclose,
A gem so pure as the diamond dew that quivered on
    the rose.

Weaving her glowing coronals, her baby song sang
    she,
The breeze chimed in, the laughing stream, and the
    bird on the old thorn tree ;
She lifted her radiant eyes to Heaven, and the spirit
    of the child
Gave forth its incense with the flowers—an offering
    undefiled !

ꝊNLY A Ƒ ACTORY ꝊHILD.

ꝊNLY a factory child,
　　From her daily toil set free,
To bask for a few brief hours
　　In the light of liberty.

A child with the brow of age,
　　Decrepit, and sad, and worn ;
A waif from the city's streets,
　　Unfriended and forlorn.

Oh, what were life and hope
　　To one who had no part
With the stream that ebbed and flowed
　　Through the city's crowded heart ?

She had dreamed of azure skies,
　　Of the song of breeze and bird—
But the whirl of the factory wheels
　　Was the only song she heard.

She had dreamed of the far-off sea,
　　The wild waves murmuring strain—
The crash of the spectral wheels
　　Still throbbing through her brain.

A shifting grain of sand
  Tossed on the stormy beach,
From the human sea too low
  For human love to reach.

A child—with wasted form,
  Distorted and shrunken limb,
Wearing no trace of youth's glad prime,
  Fleshless, and gaunt, and grim.

Ever and ever the wheels
  Spin round with a demon's speed,
As she thinks of the winding stream
  That flows through the sunny mead.

Where the snow-white lilies shine,
  And the moonbeams softly fall,
She sees but the rift of sky
  Half hid by the factory wall.

Oh ! respite fondly sought,
  Oh ! blessed, bright reprieve ;
The victim on the rack
  Some solace may receive.

A few brief joyous hours
  Away from the dismal street ;

Through the shadowy lane she hastes
With childhood's willing feet.

Gazing on tree and flower,
   She marvels if this can be
The holy land of Heaven,   ,
   Where the captive is set free!

Hark! 'tis the sky-lark's note—
   And the glistening eyes wax dim;
To her the wild bird's chant
   Sounds like an angel's hymn.

Only a factory child,
   Abject, and poor, and mean;
With the eye of faith she sees
   What we have never seen—

That wrecked and lonely waif,
   Tossed on the stormy beach,
Can hear the perfect melody
   Our ears can never reach.

Oh! sage, who read'st the stars,
   Till the waning moon turns pale,
Learn of a child to rend
   From nature's face the veil.

Watch and Wait.

Watch and wait, the tide is flowing,
    Speak not now of past defeat;
Soon the rush of struggling waters
    On the shore will chafe and beat.
Nought can stay the onward progress,
    Nor retard the march of fate;
Baffled oft, degraded never,
    Still with patience watch and wait.

All have heard the olden story—
    Bootless to recall each wrong;
Ah, we know our joys soon vanished,
    And the night of grief is long,
That with sinking hearts, and weary,
    We have watched from day to day,
Whilst the billows rolling onwards
    Only burst in showers of spray.

I know another ancient fable:
    One stood calmly on the strand,
Whilst the snowy-crested waters
    Broke upon the silvery sand;

Lingered on, though spent and weary,
   Calmly waiting day by day,
But the mournful waste of waters
   Only burst in shattered spray.

Many a passer-by derided,
   Jeered, reviled with scoffing tongue,
Taunted with insulting laughter,
   Mocked the hope to which he clung.
Not for them the higher wisdom,
   Battling bravely with defeat,
Their blinded eyes could scan no farther
   Than the waves that washed his feet.

Darkly loomed the restless ocean,
   With its wealth of buried gold ;
Every ripple on its bosom
   Over sunken treasures rolled,
Sweeping on o'er coral islands
   Gleaming pearl and rainbow gem ;
But the deep sea's cruel waters
   Void and lonely shone for them !

One by one the climbing billows
   Flung their freight upon the shore,
Pallid shells and tinted pebbles
   From the ocean's hoarded store ;

Worthless dross of scanty value,
　　Mossy seaweed, tangles brown,
Drift-wood from the foundered vessels,
　　On the slippery beach were strewn.

Watch and wait—the future neareth,
　　Chafe not over past defeat ;
The tide of time, that rolleth onward,
　　Bears its treasures to your feet :
Unexplored that mystic ocean,
　　With its hidden mine of gold—
Hope and patience may discover
　　What the NEXT wave may unfold !

A POET'S THANKSGIVING.

I THANK Thee, Father ! with a child's deep love
　　For all thy gifts to me,
Daily and hourly crowding round my path,
　　Fulfilling Thy decree.
Deem me not thankless, if the heart seems cold—
　　That heart with fervour fill—
In Iceland's frozen clime the boiling spring
　　Leaps upward at Thy will.

I bless Thee for the deep blue summer skies,
  The sunset's gleaming gold;
The azure-tinted clouds spreading afar,
  Like banners, fold on fold:
The lightning-freighted masses trailing low,
  Dark as a funeral pall;
The pale clear twilight dying in the west —
  I thank Thee, LORD, for all!

I hear the soft chime of the mountain rill,
  The skylark's matin song;
The far-off murmur of the homeward bee,
  The heathery moors among;
The music of the incense-laden breeze
  That rings the lily's bell,
Swaying the fern's green "sunburst" to and fro
  Deep in the shady dell.

A dew-drop on the fairy-haunted thorn,
  A sere leaf rippling by;
The glinting of the harvest moon that lights
  The sombre autumn sky;
The river gliding, like a path of gems,
  The lonely way-side flower;
The ivy-wreath that drapes the storied arch
  And mouldering ruined tower.

Have I not loved them, as a poet loves,
    Until the eyes ran o'er,
And the full heart, weighed down with sudden joy,
    Felt it could hold no more?
Have I not loved them? Father! not in vain
    The gorgeous feast was spread;
At bounteous nature's glorious jubilee
    The lowliest may be fed.

For me those sands that glisten in the stream
    May wear a golden hue;
The sapphire gleams amid the nestling leaves,
    And not the violet blue:
The hawthorn bough is starred with lavish pearls—
    A diamond wreath and zone
Would pale beside the rich and priceless wealth
    A poet's heart can own.

For me the rainbow's dazzling portal seems
    A grand triumphal arch,
And proudly to the tempest's trumpet call
    The unseen victors march:
The wild wave's whispered cadence, murmured low,
    The booming of the sea,
Reveal the wondrous tale—so often told ·
    Of God's infinity!

Better to cling to childhood's simple faith,
    To legends dim and old,
To deem the May-flower by the sunny stream
    A sentinel of gold !
Let the dear story of the aspen's leaf
    The listener's heart enthral—
Oh, better to believe with childlike trust
    Than not believe at all !

Father ! no ruthless hand, no tyrant power,
    Can wrest one gift away,
Nor quench the glory of the coming morn—
    Ending in perfect day !
I thank thee for the chiming mountain rill,
    The flowers that gem the sod,
The sunset sky, the skylark's song—for all
    I thank Thee, oh, my GOD !

THE CONVICT'S FLOWER.

"There is an old, old legend of a little pale blue flower, which, it is said,
blooms only on the graves of convicts."

WHO may tell their life's lost story, and their deeds
    of guilt proclaim ?
Urn, nor cross, nor sculptured column, bears one record
    of a name ;

Long forgotten, they are sleeping in the felon's ghastly
    graves—
What to them the idle sorrow that their hapless memory
    craves ?

Who may tell the dark temptations ere their footsteps
    turned astray,
With no light to guide them onward, with no hand to
    point the way ?
Ye who call their sentence justice—ah, 'tis easy to
    condemn—
Boasting vainly of your virtue—have you e'er been
    tried like them ?

Long forgotten, none to mourn them, spurned in life,
    reviled in death ;
None to guard their outlawed memory, none to shield
    from slander's breath ;
Yet one pure and sinless token decks their lowly graves
    of shame,
Though no urn nor stately column bears the record of
    a name.

Lonely flower, what hand hath reared thee ?—silent
    guardian of the dead,
Softly gleam thy pale blue petals on the convict's
    narrow bed :

Who may tell thy life's brief story—stem, and bud,
    and fragile spray?
Who hath tended, lived, and watched thy leaves un-
    folding day by day?

It may be—GOD alone can tell us—that the mouldering
    hearts beneath
Still retained some trace of beauty, only now revealed
    in death ;
And the pale flower watching o'er them, with its leaves
    of softest blue,
May be some lost virtue springing from the hearts once
    warm and true !

Words of scorn too harshly spoken may have struck
    some quivering nerve—
The good and evil of man's nature ev'n the lightest
    touch may swerve :
Skilful fingers wake rich music, careless hands but jar
    the string ;
From the chords of human passion let no tone of
    discord ring.

Love, that met with bitter hatred, chilled like flowers
    beneath the frost ;
Faith, and hope, and gentlest mercy, all like scattered
    riches lost :

Ye who seek for sunken treasures on the ocean's stormy
track,
Leave the gold and costly jewels, strive to raise the
human wreck !

Not in vain this sweet flower springeth from th' un-
consecrated sod,
Silent record of the lost ones, planted by the hand of
GOD ;
Guard the sleepers, drooping blossom, shield them
though the sky may lower—
Better far than sculptured column is the lonely con-
vict's flower !

PROUDLY WE STAND IN THE PEOPLE'S RANKS.

PROUDLY we stand in the people's ranks, to war
with the people's wrong—
Though not always the race be to the swift, the battle
to the strong ;
We dare to preach forth the branded creed of equal
rights to all—
On the evil and just will the fruitful rain and the
cheering sunbeams fall.

Our weapons—true thought and fearless speech—with
    these we will overthrow
Each low device and base pretence, each aim of the
    crafty foe ;
We laugh at their hollow sophistry, their station, rank,
    and caste,
Their senseless barricade of words our arms will soon
    lay waste.

'Tis idle to prate of rank and class—nay, urge not the
    shallow plea—
Remember who sat in the fisherman's boat on Gallilee's
    purple sea !
Rend the tyrant chains that custom forged, and recant
    the impious creed
That a separate law for rich and poor by GOD's wisdom
    was decreed.

Remember who sat at the publican's feast !—was there
    peer or noble there ?
What jewelled garter, or diamond star, did those guests,
    so honoured, wear ?
Ah, men, arise from delusion's sleep, fling off the coils
    that bind
The free-born soul's exalted strength, the heaven-
    endowèd mind,

And proudly stand in the people's ranks, to war with
    fraud and wrong :
Oh, pass not by—ye have stood apart, ye have held
    aloof too long ;
Fear not to utter the glorious faith of equal rights to
    all :
On the evil and just will the fruitful rain and the
    cheering sunbeams fall.

THE TWO INVITATIONS.

SHE hears the music of the Christmas bells,
    And gladness fills the wildly throbbing heart :
The festal hour is near, and, draped in robes
Of snowy sheen, whose gorgeous shifting folds
Are starred with many a gem, she turns aside,
A smile of rapture on her glowing lip.
Fair is that mirrored form—the auburn hair
Shot with rich gleams of gold, the pale pure brow
Decked with a coronal of radiant flowers.
Again the bells ring out, again she smiles
On the white mirrored form that meets her gaze :
She sees them all—the laughing lip, the eye
That longs to flash back looks of burning love,
To speak the silent language of the heart.

Will *he* not deem her fair, the chosen one?
For him the wreath was twined, the snowy robe
Starred with rich gems—for him the Christmas bells
Ring their glad summons through the wintry air.

Cold is the fireless hearth, the restless glare
Of the dull rush-light falls in checkered shades
On the grim garret wall, the sunken floor,
The pallet bed, where the worn sufferer rests.
She hears the solemn bells, and stills her heart
To listen to their chimes—oh, what to her
Are pain and suffering now—oh, what to her
Cold, hunger, and the world's unpitying scorn?
Before to-morrow's dawn a fairer robe
Than ever graced earth's festal scenes will clothe
Her wasted limbs—a crown, more peerless far
Than glittering gold or gems of fabled price,
Will deck the brow, damp with the dews of death.
Is *she* forsaken in that garret home,
Is there no voice to pierce the ghastly gloom,
To bid her welcome to the festal scene?
Ring out, oh, blessed bells, ring out with joy!
Well may the faded lip with rapture smile,
The dim eye glow with gratitude and love—
A Monarch's guest, she goeth home to spend
Her Christmas night amid the host of Heaven!

In the Workhouse.

Open wide the latticed window : has the spring
    already come ?
I had scarcely hoped such rapture on my weary
    journey home ;
Pleasant 'tis to meet old faces, and to feel old friends
    are near—
Bend a little lower—tell me, did you say that spring
    was here?

Sings the red-breast on the elm tree—I have heard
    that song before,
When the twilight shadows darkened, standing by my
    cabin door ;
Wider fling the lattice open, raise my head that I may
    see
The snow-drop shining on the green sward, and the
    bird upon the tree.

Do not smile with cruel pity, I am not so changed
    and weak,
Every pulse is bravely beating, though the tears are
    on my cheek ;

If the sight of bird and blossom this poor stricken
    heart can move,
Blame me not, but, oh, remember I have little left to
    love !

Still the old and thread-bare fable—cease that hollow
    lying cant,
Tell me not that food and shelter can supply my every
    want ;
Stifling in this pauper dungeon, guarded by that pon-
    derous wall,
Housed, like jaded, worn-out cattle, each can claim
    his ghastly stall.

Could the past be but forgotten, even I might cease
    to crave
Aught beyond this workhouse palace, and the pauper's
    nameless grave :
Hark ! upon the roof descending, falls like lead the
    plashing rain—
Am I dreaming? 'tis the tolling of the bell that strikes
    my brain.

Hark ! I hear the children's voices, not the voices of
    the dead,
O'er their graves the leaves of autumn in their crimson
    glow were shed ;

You never saw my gentle Ellen—God be thanked, she
    was set free,
And the gloomy prison portals only opened wide for
    me.

For myself, it matters little, I have endless sorrows
    borne,
But to think the parish raiment by my darling should
    be worn ;
Better die of knawing hunger, lacking even daily bread,
Than the lips I loved so dearly by cold charity be fed.

Close the window, night is falling, the robin's evening
    song is o'er,
Blotted out the sunset shadows dancing on the glaring
    floor :
Bend your head down to the pillow—did you tell me
    spring was come ?
I am cold and very weary, and I long to hasten home.

THE BOAT WRECK.

"THE wind has sunk—'twas a pitiless night—
    Thank God that the morn is come ;
What news ? oh, tell me, and tell me true,
    Have the fishermen's boats come home ?

E

I have wept and watched through the long drear hours.
  With a trembling ghastly fear,
Longing to know the awful truth ;
  Longing, yet dreading to hear.

" You say they have all returned ? who cares
  For the hurricane's deadly crash,
Let the wild winds rave, and the thunder boom,
  And the blinding lightning flash :
The sea, like a baffled fiend, may fling
  Aloft its scattered spray ;
We can mock its power when the fishermen's craft
  Is anchored in the bay !

" Hark ! 'tis a footstep—no, 'tis gone,
  And my heart beats loud and wild ;
But the pitiless blast has died away,
  The ocean has spared my child—
The last lamb of the stricken fold,
  Sole star of my darkening sky,
My only son—my golden haired,
  The light of the widow's eye.

" Why does he tarry ? the slow hours fade,
  And he so fleet of limb ?
Oh, none can row with so trusty a hand,
  Or trim a sail with him :

When the drowning shrieks were heard along
  The ocean's pathless track,
He was the first to stem the wave,
  The last to leave the wreck !

" When I hear the whispering waters break
  Upon the shingly strand,
I sometimes think 'tis a far-off voice
  From another, better land.
Husband and first-born, both went down,
  Gorged by the hungry sea ;
Yet, Heaven be praised, one joy remains—
  My son is left to me !

" When the dying day burned in the west,
  The seven good boats set sail,
With a chosen band of stalwart men
  Who had weathered many a gale ;
But the bravest, truest, best of all
  Was Brian, the widow's son—
And you say that the fleet have all returned ?"
  " Aye, woman, all save *one !*

" Save one ?   Oh, God ! where is the boat
  That followed in the wake ?"
" Rent in twain on the bristling crags
  Where the boiling billows break."

"And the crew?"   "All lost from stem to stern :
    Nay, woman, ask no more—
When the buried dead arise, the sea
    Will yield its hidden store."

"Again I hear the whispering waves
    Break gently on the strand,
Another voice—another from
    The far-off spirit land :
Husband and children, all, all gone,
    Gorged by the hungry sea ;
The ocean holds my buried dead,
    And none are left to me.

"The wind has sunk—'twas a fearful night,
    But the cold pale morn is come ;
I cannot tell—but I think he said
    That *six* of the fleet came home—
Where is the boat that followed last,
    Where is my boy—my son?
Oh, GOD ! Thou knowest the awful truth,
    They have all returned save ONE !"

Under the Orchard Tree.

Under the orchard trees unseen, alone
 She sadly lingers—shadows undefined,
Hopes, doubts, and fears, uncertainty, suspense,
By turns blot out the sunshine from her soul.
Fair is the scene—it bears no charm for her :
She sees no beauty in the glowing flowers
That cluster round her feet ; no radiance dwells
Within the fox-glove's bells ; no sweetness fills
The violet's purple gem ; the robin sings
Its witching song in vain ; the soul untuned
Discerns no melody in nature's voice.

Under the sheltering trees, *not now* alone,
She lingers fondly—thoughts strange, undefined,
Joy, faith, heart-peace, and happiness,
Like summer sunshine, flood her wakened soul.
Fair is the scene—to her how passing fair !
What magic beauty decks the starry flowers
That cluster at her feet : the fairy bells,
Trembling upon the breeze like eastern gems,
Ring forth triumphant tones ; the violet's leaf
Unfolds a wealth of sweetness ; amethysts
Gleam where so late the purple clover bloomed ;

Soft breezes ripple 'mid the leafy boughs,
And shell-like petals deck the lustrous head
Bowed 'neath a very agony of joy !
Hark to that witching music—how her heart
Beats time to the soft measure, lip and eye
Lit with a smile of triumph : never yet
Did tropic bird, with wings of azure sheen,
Carol so sweet a strain !

Under the shadowy trees, with arms entwined,
And true hand locked in hand they linger still ;
For them sweet nature holds a jubilee,
And spreads a banquet for love-sated hearts !

The Artificial Flower Maker.

Heavily roll the cheerless hours in their incessant
    flight,
Bringing no morn of happiness, but night, still endless
    night ;
With sorrow, want, and wretchedness, no hope, no
    change for me,
Till God, in mercy, sends to set the toil-worn captive
    free.

Little they think of the weary slave who twines the
 festal wreath—
Each garland these wasted fingers weave but brings
 me nearer death ;
Yet I love to look on the rainbow hues, as I fashion
 the gem-like flowers,
In their meek beauty live again the blossoms of childhood's hours.

The wreaths that my infant hands once wove, when
 my trembling footsteps trod
In search of those dear loved treasures, which I then
 deemed gifts from GOD !
There is not a bud nor a leaf I form but seems to my
 aching gaze
Like the faded flowers o'er whose early death I wept
 in other days.

These glittering bands of roses, how gracefully they
 wave,
Yet lovelier far the blossoms that decked my mother's
 grave !
When the gentle petals closing on the cross lay down
 to die,
I fed them with my heart's best tears in speechless
 misery.

See'st thou these starry violets?—my little sister's eyes
Could boast a deeper azure than their blue resplendent
  dyes;   .
And that white and radiant lily, outrivalling the snow,
Is not more beautiful and pure than her unclouded
  brow.

They said that my own cheek wore a blush, deep as
  the rose-bud's heart,
That never to glowing lip did health a brighter hue
  impart;
But now I fear to lift my eyes, to gaze on the face that
  gleams
From the broken mirror on my wall, so sorrowful it
  seems.

So sorrowful and sad it seems, my heart nigh breaks
  to see
The image of our own GOD defaced by want and
  poverty;
The pallid cheek, and the hollow eye, and the brow
  so dark with pain,
I think that each glance will be my last, yet still look
  up again.

When my pale hands garland the " orange flowers" in
    many a circling wreath,
I sigh to think that the bridal crown is fanned by the
    breath of death ;
I would not that my falling tears should sully one
    trembling spray,
So I try to cheer me for the task, and brush my tears
    away.

I try to wear on my altered lip the semblance of a
    smile,
And I sing some olden melody the dreary time to
    while ;
Ye know not how sad and lone it is to toil in this
    darkened room,
Whilst the shadows gleam like spectres in the dim
    and ghastly gloom.

Ye know not how sad and lone it is to labour with
    tortured brain,
Until the bent and weary limbs are quivering with
    pain ;
To see the produce of your toil, chaplet, and wreath,
    and band,
At the word of fashion coldly spurned, as the work of
    an *Irish* hand !

So I pine in hopeless misery, no solace need I crave,
No help for the wretched captive, no help for the
  Irish slave !
When pity, love, and tenderness return to the hearts
  of men,
Then may I hope for mercy—but never until then.

There's a Storm far out at Sea.

There's a storm far out at sea—
 Where the light-house lamp burns bright,
 Through the long cold hopeless night;
 And the vengeful waves leap out
 With a fierce exultant shout ;
 Like a falling meteor's gleam
 The fitful flashes stream,
 Till the buried gems below
 Shine out in the fiery glow.

There's a fierce storm out at sea—
 Pale faces peer in vain
 From the lighted cabin pane ;

The blinding snow sweeps on,
Earth, ocean—all are gone :
I hear the boatman's oar,
As he makes for the sheltering shore—
Hark ! 'tis but the savage sea
Laughing in cruel mockery.

It blows a fresh'ning gale—
The life-boat on the beach
The drowning ship may reach :
Come, launch the gallant craft,
And man her fore and aft ;
The light in the cabin pane
Will guide us back again.
Hark ! 'tis the signal gun—away,
Our brothers perish whilst we stay.

There's a wild storm on the land—
Alas, no saving light
Gleams 'mid *our* dreary night :
The winds may chafe and rave,
No hand is stretched to save ;
Fell anarchy and hate
Have left us desolate—
The minute gun may boom in vain,
No answer meets the sad refrain.

There's a rough gale on the land—
   Rancour and envious scorn
   Render our homes forlorn.
   What are the storms that sweep
   The bosom of the deep,
   To the pitiless blasts that rend
   True loving friend from friend?
   Better the billows' threatening roar
   Than the raging tempest on the shore!

There's a fierce storm on the land—
   Oh, foot that trod the wave,
   Thou that alone can'st save,
   Haste to our foundering barque,
   Haste, for the skies grow dark:
   When the maddening storms beat high,
   Oh, list to our struggling cry;
   Bend the wild tempest to Thy will,
   And speak the blessed words, "Be still!"

THE STAG HUNT.

ONWARD, rushing wildly forth,
　　With feet that seem to spurn the earth,
Over mountain, rock, and crag,
Swiftly flies the hunted stag !
Through the glen and haunted brake,
Where a thousand echoes wake ;
Sweeping o'er the new-mown meadow,
Noiseless as a creeping shadow :
On, with every sinew straining,
(Now the fearful pass 'tis gaining)
And the beagles madly follow
Through the lonely mountain hollow.
One brief pause, one glance behind,
Away, then, fleeter than the wind ;
With heaving breast, and swelling vein,
And limbs that could not brook a chain !
The rushing stream is gained, 'tis passed—
A moment, and the hounds have crossed !
A moment yet—oh ! fleeter still
The wild deer climbs the rugged hill ;
With dauntless front one look is cast
Upon the foes that follow fast—
Away again : it seems to breast
The clouds that screen the eagle's nest !

Each chasm, gorge, and cleft, it clears—
But, hark! the foremost beagle nears;
A crash, an onward sweep, a bound,
The spreading antlers touch the ground.
One effort more, though hope seems gone,
The forest child still hurries on
To win the paltry boon of life—
'Tis scarcely worth so dread a strife!
But yet the wearied limbs disdain
The pressure of the servile chain:
One effort more—the quivering flank
Lies on the ground all cold and dank!
With curdling blood, and glazing eye,
The wounded stag is left to die!
The hand had missed that struck the blow,
An erring finger pulled the bow!
There's strength in every limb, though chill,
The pulse of life is throbbing still.
Again the proud heart boundeth free,
With hopes of coming liberty;
And visions of the future rise
To chase the clouds from those soft eyes.
Oh! for a chance of freedom yet,
Before the autumn's sun hath set,
The maddening race to run again;
Perhaps the " stricken deer" might gain!

THE AMERICAN LETTER.

They waited in silent deep suspense,
　Till the old man broke the seal;
Each quivering lip and brow told more
　Than words could e'er reveal.

He broke the seal with a trembling hand,
　Whilst the crowd still onward pressed,
And those who were nearest could hear the sobs
　That burst from his aged breast.

He strove to speak, but no sound arose,
　Save the low wail of despair;
He looked once more on the opened page,
　But hope was murdered there.

And, oh! it was piteous to see the head—
　White as the *ceanabhan's* snow—
Crushed to the earth with the heavy grief,
　And the broken heart's wild woe!

But the fearful storm of his soul passed by,
　As a gust o'er the forest oak;
And, wrestling with his agony,
　The old man slowly spoke—

" Father, she pined like a wounded bird,
    Growing fainter day by day ;
  But her closing eyes still fondly turned
    To the old land far away.

"To her own loved home 'neath the fairy thorn,
    On the green hill's gentle brow—
  They say that the hearth is quenched and cold,
    And the roof-tree lying low.

"She used to sing in the star-lit eve—
    Oh, father, *that* song you know,
  That rose each night in our golden tongue,
    In the old time, long ago.

"We may not tell, for what hand could write
    Of the anguish, deep and strong,
  That came, like the sweep of the tempest's might,
    With the tones of our sister's song.

"We may not tell how we strove to hide
    From our Nora's dying gaze
  The grief that our darling strove to soothe
    With those wild heart-breaking lays.

"Yet still she pined, like a stricken bird,
    And we thought it strange to see

" The cheek grows pale that had never changed
    In the days of poverty.

" And the foot, so light in the lone bohreen,
    Fell heavy, and faint, and slow ;
  For, oh, there's no weight that will crush you down
    Like the heart oppressed with woe !

" In her new-made grave she is sleeping now—
    Oh, father, *asthore !* weep on ;
  It will ease your heart, though it can't recall
    The darling that's dead and gone.

" Send us, to strew o'er her gentle breast,
    The flowers that she loved so well :
  Father·! the shamrock, you'll not forget,
    That grows in the hawthorn dell !

" Oh, what to her were the grand old woods,
    And the flowers of dazzling sheen ?
  Better one spray from the rowan tree
    That shadows the village green !

" Though the forest boughs were of purest gold,
    And every leaf a gem,
  Dearer the bud on our wild rose tree,
    Now mouldering on the stem !

F

" Father, the empty dream is gone—
  Oh, God ! for the bitter waking—
This foreign home is no home for us
  While the desolate heart is breaking.

" Home ? with the grief that eats out life,
  Like a worm at the apple's core ;
No joy for us until we forget
  The days that are past and o'er.

" What care we for these glowing skies,
  And the prairie rolling wide ?
We know where the moonbeams slumber now—
  Afar on a green hill side.

" Tell us how prospers the ancient land—
  Are her days of plenty come ?
Oh, many a heart is yearning here
  For tidings from our home.

" Hurrah for the eve when we'll meet once more
  By our own hearth's cheering glow,
And gently speak, as one speaks of the dead,
  Of the old time long ago.

" Hurrah !"—but the old man's voice grew faint :
  What to him was gladness now ?

He only thought of the foreign grave
   Where the child of his love lay low.

He folded the letter and turned away :
   And his purpose no one knew,
Till he bent his steps to the hawthorn dell
   Where the symbol shamrocks grew.

The Pilgrim at the Well.

Sowly she kneeled by the sainted well,
   The dew of night o'er her dark hair fell ;
She-lifted her face to the midnight skies,
Not a star appeared to those sightless eyes :
Not a ray of hope to her heart was given,
Yet, she meekly bowed to the will of Heaven ;
And the mother gazed on her darling child,
As she kneeled in that lone and dreary wild.
Again she strove o'er her brow to fling
The sparkling foam of the holy spring,
Again she cast on the starry skies
The flashing gleam of those sightless eyes ;
With a bursting heart then turned aside
The burning tear of despair to hide.

In silence they roamed on their weary way,
Till their cabin dwelling before them lay;
Glad voices of joy on the breeze are borne,
The mother and child to their home return;
The light step of childhood comes bounding by,
And a welcome shines from each laughing eye—
"We have piled fresh wood on our cabin hearth,
See, Morna! see how the red blaze leaps forth;
Sister, there's light in thy gleaming eyes,
No darkening cloud on their splendour lies."
The cheerful glow on her pale face fell,
She saw not the forms she loved so well;
And the blind girl wept o'er her hapless lot,
As she turned away from that treasured spot.
"I have sought, 'mid our little garden bowers,
For the greenest leaves and the fairest flowers,
And a pale and shadowy wreath I wove
To twine round the cage of your captive dove;
On its dazzling wing doth a violet rest,
And a rose-leaf gleams from its snowy breast:
Look, Morna, look on its proud bright eye,
It glows in the light of the morning sky!"
But Morna saw not the gentle bird,
Her head was bowed, and her heart was stirred;
The cloud of despair on her spirit pressed
Like a heavy shower on a young flower's breast!

Her head was bowed that they might not trace
The darkened gloom of her altered face ;
But a fearful vision came o'er them now,
As she pressed her lips to each spotless brow.
In vain, in vain did the bright fire blaze,
Ne'er could it meet her darkened gaze.
She heard the coo of her gentle dove,
But saw not the wreath they had round it wove ;
She knew that the eyes she loved were near,
For her cheek was wet with an infant's tear !
And she heard the burst of the heavy sigh,
As they wept in their bitter agony—
But the blind girl smiled, for a light from Heaven
In that trying hour to her heart was given !

A HOME.

LOOK upon this household picture—has the limner
    painted true,
Are the lights too warmly blended, are the shades too
    deep in hue ?
Untaught hands record the vision little skilled in artist's
    lore,
Wayward fancy's magic pencil paints from memory's
    choicest store.

I can see thy southern dwelling, 'mid the flowers we
    love so well,
Fondly twines each drooping blossom, opening bud
    and trembling bell;
Clustering round thy cottage windows starry gems like
    rubies gleam,
Brighter than the golden splendour of the sunset's
    parting beam.

I can see the tall trees swaying in thin garb of freshest
    green,
Softly fall the flitting shadows on the flowers of dazzling
    sheen—
Hark! the south winds aerial music wakes each quiver-
    ing leaf and spray,
Like a burst of childish laughter rings the breeze's
    minstrelsy.

Who can fetter fancy's pinion? thought is strong, and
    wild, and free—
I can tell where spring the violets 'neath the fairy
    haunted tree—
Where the fern's green banner waveth, nature's "sun-
    burst" still unrolled,
Many a pensive primrose bloometh with its leaves of
    palest gold!

Hearest thou not yon wild bird warbling in the soft
    arbutus grove ?
Listen to the liquid music, to the artless song of love ;
As the murmur of a brooklet, gushes forth the glad-
    dening lay—
Songster, taught of God and nature, sing thy welcome
    to the May.

Listen—from the dim old forest grander melodies
    arise,
Like a trumpet's stormy music pealing proudly to the
    skies ;
Never yet did holier anthem greet us in the sacred
    fane,.
Than the bird's soft melting carol, and the wind's
    triumphant strain !

Like a shower of shivered diamonds glancing 'mid the
    bending trees,
Onward floats the grand old river with its storied
    memories —
Onward by the shadowy woodland, by the rath, the
    keep, and tower,
Dim memorials of past greatness, records of a prouder
    hour.

POEMS:

Onward, like a path of silver, by the ruined abbey
    wall,
By the cabin's shattered roof-tree (none are left to
    mourn its fall) ;
By the shamrock-spangled meadow, where the glisten-
    ing May-flowers shine—
Seem they not like jewelled treasures from the fairy's
    golden mine.

Look upon this household picture—has the limner
    painted true,
Are the lights too warmly blended, and the shades too
    deep in hue ?
Untaught hands record the vision, little skilled in
    artist's lore,
Wayward fancy's magic pencil paints from memory's
    choicest store !

THE ANGEL'S MESSAGE.

"There is a beautiful belief in the East, that flowers form the alphabet of
angels, by which they communicate their thoughts to man."

By the lone way side bending, by fairy rath and
    stream,
The fairest jewels of the earth in pictured beauty
    gleam ;

A mirrored rainbow seems to light the sward on hill
    and fell,
And gems of radiant loveliness glow from each hidden
    dell.

The holy wells are garlanded with flowers of rarest
    sheen,
O'er storied arch and ruined pile wave chaplets fresh
    and green ;
The ivy drapery curtaineth the mouldering keep and
    tower
As lovingly as if the wreaths twined round a sylvan
    bower.

What wóndrous love each bud reveals—each chalice
    brimmed with dew :
Oh, solemn flowers ! earth's wisest ones had need to
    learn of you ;
The winds that sway the .fern's light plume some
    weird-like tale may tell,
And angel-thoughts peal softly from the hyacinth's
    pure bell.

Deep in the emerald meadows rich traceries of gold,
Blending with snow-white blossoms, their secret wealth
    unfold ;

And, gently, with her perfumed breath the violet waves
    us back
To search amid the heaped-up leaves that strew the
    forest's track.

What magic words are written with the tendrils of the
    vine,
The leaves o'er which the sunbeams play some charmèd
    lore enshrine ;
The "lily of the valley's" pearls that tremble on the
    spray,
So soft and pure, would well beseem an angel's rosary !

Oh ! not in vain we lingering pause, to scan with
    wondering eyes
The mystic characters engraved on gems of varied
    dyes ;
No need to seek in ponderous tome, nor ask of seer
    or sage,
A key to con the simple truths on nature's glorious
    page.

Fling wide the factory doors, and bid the children
    cease from toil,
The chains of earth were never forged around young
    hearts to coil ;

Unbar the prison gates, and let the hapless captives
  come—
For them, for us, the flowers have brought a message
  from our home !

Look where they cluster round our path—wan toilers :
  come away,
The rippling breeze is showering down rich blossoms
  of the May,
The fox-gloves belfry softly rings a welcome faint and
  clear,
But at the pealing of those chimes no elfin tribes
  appear.

By the lone way-side bending, by fairy rath and
  stream,
The angel's pictured characters like costly jewels
  gleam ;
Each leaf that trembles in the breeze, each flower that
  gems the sod,
Will teach the heart, though crushed and worn, to love
  and worship GOD !

J HAVE ┼OVED THEE.

(From the Irish.)

J HAVE loved thee, dear and fond one,
  With a pure unchanging love ;
Teach, oh, teach me thou canst only
  How that tenderness to prove.

Let me soothe thine hours of sadness,
  When the world seems false and cold,
And thy heart is weary—I can
  Bring thee rarer wealth than gold.

Here, on this fond breast reclining,
  I shall kiss away each tear ;
Whilst a true heart throbs beside thee,
  What hast thou, beloved, to fear ?

Worn with toil, come, rest thee, darling—
  Gaze upon me with those eyes ;
Looks of deepest love shall greet thee,
  Smiles as soft as April skies.

If the hand of sickness smite thee,
　Who will tend with gentler care,
And, forgetting her own sorrows,
　Only ask *thy* griefs to share?

Who will feel such exultation
　When each tongue proclaims thy praise,
And the favoured child of genius
　Basks in fortune's cloudless blaze?

Summer's roses twine around us,
　Summer's sunshine glints above;
Life seems nought but flowers and brightness.
　‑Joy, and extacy, and love.

If the drooping garlands wither,
　And the sunbeams fade away—
Not for us the scattered blossoms,
　Not for us the darkening day.

I have loved thee, and thee only,
　With a pure unchanging love—
Even a life-time were too fleeting
　All my tenderness to prove!

EVANGELINE.

SHE stood in the jessamine-wreathed porch—the
    ringing laugh was stilled,
A speechless dread and sudden awe her infant spirit
    filled ;
The dewy eyes were raised to Heaven, with child-
    hood's trusting love,
As she thought of that wondrous story—the descent
    of the Holy Dove !

She stood in the flower-enwreathèd porch, 'mid blos-
    soms bright and fair,
A spray of the wild "forget-me-not" half hid in the
    sunny hair ;
And ever she gazed with childhood's faith afar through
    the pathless track,
With the folded Bible in her hands, waiting to give it
    back.

A purple cloud, begirt with gold, uprose in the glowing
    west,
Spreading out cumbrous fold on fold, like a banner's
    gorgeous crest ;

But the radiant splendour died away, the glittering
    flag was furled,
And the darkened shades of the solemn night came
    down on the silent world.

She thought of the city's sapphire walls, of the burning
    sea of glass,
As she gazed on the feathery wreaths of clouds piled
    up in a snowy mass ;
Of the shining gates of orient pearl, and almost hoped
    to see
The harpers harping, and to hear their songs of
    victory.

They had told her the Bible was GOD's own book,
    and she deemed it a bitter wrong
That the precious treasure lent by Him should be
    retained so long ;
And ever she waited with patient hope, till the sad-
    dened face grew pale,
To think that the story heard so oft should prove but
    an idle tale.

Oh, that some angel, sent by GOD, a message of love
    would bring :
Hark ! 'tis only the rustling sound of a bird on home-
    ward wing.

Surely from all the host of Heaven a white-robed saint
    might come,
Cleaving the space amid the stars, to take the Bible
    home !

Waiting for God, she lingered still, while the shadows
    of evening fell,
And ever she held in her baby-hand the Book that
    she loved so well ;
Though the violet eyes were dimmed with tears, and
    the saddened face grew pale,
She knew that the story heard so oft could not be an
    idle tale.

WORSHIP.

COME, the summer morn is dawning, brothers, sisters,
    come away,
Holy hands have reared the temple—we must worship
    there to-day :
The wild bird sings a joyous welcome—list yon carol
    loved so well,
To your ears, poor weary toilers, sounding like a
    sabbath bell.

From the factory, from the workshop, from the crowded
    garret come,
Gaze, with eyes and hearts o'erflowing, on the picture
    of your home—
Your far-off home—deem not we mock you with a
    hope too fair and bright ;
Through the shadows that surround you softly gleams
    the morning's light.

From the dark and reeking cellar, haste, the summer
    day's begun,
Many a sight and sound shall greet you ere the setting
    of the sun :
True enjoyment is true worship, gratitude the heart's
    best prayer—
'Mid the haunts of deepest beauty, humbly kneel, for
    GOD is there.

Gaze upon this gorgeous temple, on this consecrated
    shrine,
Decked with nature's choicest treasures, fashioned by
    a hand divine ;
No fretted roof, or painted window, meets the dim and
    toil-worn eye,
But the rainbow's dazzling glory, and the deep blue
    summer's sky.

See the lily's ivory petals brimming o'er with midnight
    dew,
Never did the sculptor's chisel mould a font of fairer
    hue ;
Look upon the showy chalice quivering on the slender
    stem,
Seems it like a pearl just fallen from a royal diadem.

Here we worship, lowly kneeling on the flower-ena-
    melled sod,
Banned nor barred the portal leading to this temple
    of our GOD ;
'Mid the haunts of deepest beauty, faith forbids us to
    despair—
True enjoyment is true worship, gratitude the heart's
    best prayer !

A TALE OF THE PAST.

SHE sees the sunset melt from heaven,
    The shadowy twilight fall,
The pale cold moon come sailing up
    To whiten the castle wall.

The pale, cold moon come sailing up,
    Like a far-off ship at sea,
Drifting, amid the island clouds,
    One star upon the lea.

The belfry tower looms overhead—-
    She listens with baited breath!
Hark to the warning peal that breaks
    A silence deep as death.

Hark !—but the changing tones are mute,
    The evening breeze sweeps on ;
The bells will ring a louder peal
    Before to-morrow's dawn.

The bells will ring a louder peal
    As the priests, with hood and stole,
Chant a sad *miserere*
    For the convict's passing soul.

The headsman's stroke falls swift and true,
    The axe is bright and keen—
The noblest blood in all the land
    Will dim its glittering sheen.

She stands by the prison's grisly walls,
    Footsore and all forlorn ;

A cry breaks from her parted lips
    As she thinks of the coming morn.

An eerie cry, like the tortured wail
    Of an arrow-stricken deer,
And the bursting heart with anguish throbs
    As the fearful end draws near.

Oh, cold and pale the weird-like moon,
    As she moves in solemn state ;
But colder the white uplifted face
    That leans by the prison gate.

Blinded and stunned by despair's fell blow,
    She heeds not the passing hour,
Till the fitful chimes ring out again
    From the castle's belfry tower.

Then the slumbering strength of a maddened soul
    Came back like the tide's full flow—
With the deathless might of a woman's love
    She would parry the fatal blow.

On the iron-girded door she knocked,
    With a firm untrembling hand ;
Her voice had a strange unwonted tone,
    As she uttered her stern demand.

Bright gold was offered—the gold was scorned,
　Rare gems—but 'twas in vain ;
Not the diamond's blaze, nor the ruby's glow,
　Could sever the captive's chain.

Her eyes flashed out with a sudden glare—
　She would bide there until morn ;
The way was long, the night was chill—
　She was desolate and forlorn.

From her hands each dazzling ring she took,
　From her bosom a perling rare—
The sparkling jewels glimmered bright
　In the flickering lamp's faint glare.

Fain would she part with that peerless hoard
　For only one fleeting hour
With her lord, who was doomed to die at morn
．　In the castle's fatal tower.

A muffled footstep nears his cell—
　Oh, moment of radiant bliss :
Little she cares for the diamond's blaze
　As her lips receive his kiss.

Oh, for the sad long gaze of love
　That met her pitying eye,
As together they watch through the window bars
　For morning in the sky.

Oh, for the wailing cry that pierced
    The dismal gloom of night :
One parting kiss—one clasp—ere dawns
    That morning's hateful light.

Stealthily from the dungeon cell
    A muffled step glides on,
The gate swings wide on its creaking hinge,
    But the fugitive is gone.

The headsman whets the gleaming axe,
    His brawny arms are bare ;
He hears the clang of the passing bell
    Resound through the misty air.

He hears the tramp of the funeral train,
    The onward tread to death—
Oh, never did conqueror prouder march
    To win the victor's wreath.

By the murderer's block the martyr stands,
    While the mass is faintly sung ;
And a hurried prayer for the passing soul
    Ascends from every tongue.

A crimson glow on the pale cheek burned,
    The eye flashed proud and free :—

" Little ye thought on the eagle's perch
 A timid dove to see !

" Little ye dreamed that a woman's love
 Could rend the tyrant's chain :
I dare to die for my fatherland,
 If a victim must be slain.

" I scorn your threats, your baffled-ire—
 Go, search for your ransomed prey :
The noblest blood in all the land
 Will *not* be shed to-day !"

Proudly she passed through the fortress gate,
 With a stately step and slow ;
The dauntless might of a woman's love
 Had parried the fatal blow.

AGNES.

THIS is the picture : do you think it like?
 She sits beneath the lamp-light's tempered glow :
Does not the semblance of the sweet face strike?—
 Here are the dewy eyes, the pale pure brow,
The meek appealing gaze, more sad than tears,
Moving our hearts with untold trembling fears.

Soft music mingled with the fragrant air,
 Rich with the spoils of summer—bud and spray,
And leaves of brightest sheen were scattered there—
 Gleaming like jewels in the mellow ray :
The solemn chords our listening spirits stirred,
But more than earthly melodies *she* heard !

Oh, could it be that other strains chimed in,
 Blending with our imperfect harmonies ?
The golden harp, tones of the cherubin,
 And song of triumph from the starry skies—
We saw the glowing lip with joy grow pale,
The rapturous eyes that pierced beyond the veil !

We did not know GOD's angel's were so near-
 GOD's pitying angels, with white wings outspread ;
She trembled not, for love had cast out fear,
 As the strong pinions drooped above her head.
The lamb that shivered in the wintry blast
Held the blest summons to the fold at last !

On the wild wave no sounds our ears could reach,
 Tossing amid the ocean, far from home ;
Oh, not for us the shore, the welcome beach,
 Only the sunken reef, and blinding foam :
But Agnes heard the shallop touch the strand,
The ripple break upon the silver sand !

Oh, erring judgment! blindly did we mourn
 That summer's gifts for her would never shine;
For this we bid the weary feet return,
 The glad enfranchised soul in bondage pine.
Nor purple skies, nor wild bird's blythesome strain,
Nor radiant flowers could forge anew the chain!

This is her picture! these the dove-like eyes
 Subdued and soft, beneath the lamp-light's glow;
All, all of her that we were wont to prize—
 Oh, gaze once more upon the pale pure brow,
The fond imploring glance, more sad than tears,
That stirred our hearts with untold trembling fears.

The Burial of the Flower.

She knew the flower must die—the pale pure rose
 So gently tended by those infant hands:
Oh, if her love could but restore its bloom,
Reclaim the withering petals from decay,
Impart fresh vigour to the blighted stem.
'Twas her sole treasure, and the child's glad heart
Pulsed with true rapture as the perfect mass
Of gleaming whiteness met her ravished eye.

Yet day by day the taint yet deeper grew,
The burnished leaves drooped sadly from the stalk,.
And the rich odour of the doomèd flower
Waxed faint and chill.
'Twas hard, aye, passing hard, to thus resign
The heart's sole idol, never more to feast
Her eager eyes on that imperial flower ;
To know that love nor skill could yet avail
To bring back life to the pale shrivelled spray.
She knew the flower was dead—that ne'er again
The stricken leaves should wear a silvery tint,
Or yield the odour of their incense breath.
Pondering beside the cold remains, she thought
" Can such rare beauty be for ever lost,
Must the sere leaves but moulder into dust,
And the pure essence of the rose's heart
Melt like a tone of music in the air ?
What if another flower, more lovely still,
From the wan petals should up springing bloom !"
Gathering the scattered leaves with loving care,
She scooped a little grave and laid them down,
With fitting reverence covering o'er the sward,
And sprinkling many a bud of rainbow hue
On the white rose's lonely resting place.
Oh, could we but resign with childlike faith
Our hearts best idols ; could we but discard
Pale fear, and cold mistrust, and carping doubt,

And human reason's weak and treacherous aid.
Could we but lay our treasures in the dust,
Believing that a flower of fairer growth
From the cold relics should up springing bloom !

In Memoriam.

(ON THE DEATH OF A CHILD'S CANARY.)

DEAD in the flush of summer—still and cold,
    Beneath the deep-hued purple sky of June—
The sweet song hushed, the clear eye closed in sleep,
And fragile wing furled like a flower at eve.
Believe that He who marks the sparrow's fall
With gentle hand untied the silver cord,
And quenched the life so delicate and pure.
The story of our infant days reversed—
The weird old tale of babies in the wood,
With robin redbreasts for their funeral train :
But now the *bird* lies dead, and childhood weeps
Above the empty cage ; and loving hands
Fold the dear favourite in its tiny grave,
Building a monument of fragrant flowers—
A cenotaph of summer's richest gems !

LEWIE GORDON.

"Oh, send Lewie Gordon hame!"

"To arms, to arms, and we'll meet the foe
  Afar on Culloden's hill,
Whilst our hands can wield the stout claymore
  There is hope for Scotland still.

"Let the clansmen march in their serried ranks,
  And strike the final blow;
Though many a combat has been lost,
  We'll try a braver throw.

"I hear the pibroch's rallying march
  Resound through the rocky glen,
And the measured tramp of the mountain band
  Who will fight for our cause like men.

"The eagle's plumes are waving free,
  And the pennon streams on high;
Oh, shriller sounds the pibroch's notes
  As we haste to victory.

"Come on, for Lewie Gordon calls,
  And never a man shall say
That coward loon, or craven churl,
  Has led your hosts to-day!

" On—for the hated southern hordes
 Through yon dark defile have passed ;
Their trumpet peals, from crag to crag
 Rings out the echoing blast.

" Though heaven were scarcely wide enough
 Their ranks to canopy,
And they stood as thick as blades of grass,
 Our's will the triumph be !

" Come on, my trusty warriors, haste—
 To strike the final blow :
The GOD of battles nerve each arm
 Against our country's foe."

The blow was struck, the field was lost !—
 A band of gallant men
Swore by the holy cross to try
 The conflict once again.

" When the harvest moon lights up the sky
 Will Lewie Gordon come,
To lead the patriot band once more—
 To strike for GOD and home."

With bended knee, and folded hands,
 And pale brow raised to Heaven,

He vowed that only by his sword
    Should Scotland's chains be riven.

The harvest moon has passed the full,
    And days and weeks have flown;
Another moon is in the sky,
    And the conflict not begun.

And ever as the days go by,
    Strong men turn pale with dread,
And pallid lips will trembling ask—
    " Has Lewie Gordon fled ?

" Has Lewie Gordon played us false ?
    He promised back to come
And lead out Scotland's chivalry
    To strike for GOD and home."

Oh, faithless hearts, trust on—events
    Are vainly shaped by man ;
The Great Creator perfects all,
    Despite our erring plan.

The hope deferred may not be lost,
    The vow too rashly spoken
May be redeemed another time—
    The oath may not be broken.

Mankind must bend to circumstance,
   Though thought and will be free ;
No mortal power can change the laws
   That mould our destiny.

Another harvest moon may shine
   On the fields of ripening grain,
E'er Lewie Gordon come again
   Another moon may wane.

KINMONT WILLIE.

"The rescue of Kinmont Willie from Carlisle Castle by the bold Buccleuch was a daring exploit. Queen Elizabeth demanded of him how he had dared to undertake an enterprise so desperate and presumptuous? 'What is it,' replied the undaunted chieftain, 'that a man dare not do?' Elizabeth, struck with his boldness, turned to a lord in waiting, and said, 'With ten thousand such men our brother of Scotland might shake the firmest throne in Europe.'"

Oh ! cold and mirk fell the winter's night
   On Carlisle's castle towers,
As the warders paced their dreary rounds
   Through the silent mournful hours.

They heard the rain, and they heard the storm,
   And the clash of the stinging hail,
As it smote on the ancient dungeon keep
   Like the stroke of the threshing flail.

And faster fell the drifting rain,
  And louder roared the blast,
Yet never a gleam of moon nor stars
  From the ebon sky was cast.

In his prison cell, 'neath the castle towers,
  Brave Kinmont Willie lay—
The chase was o'er, and the hunted stag
  The victors held at bay.

He heard the hurricane's onward sweep,
  And a merry laugh laughed he—
" By the holy-rood, 'tis a fearful night,
  To quit this hostelrie !"

He heard the warder's distant step
  Resound through the corridor—
" I'll give them a chase," said the rebel bold
  When the prison clock chimes four !"

" Let them weave their tangled web of fraud,
  If the meshes were wrought with gold
There's never a castle in Cumberland
  Could Kinmont Willie hold !"

Hark ! there's a step on the turret stair,
  The metal door swings wide—

" Oh ! welcome, welcome, my henchmen true,"
    Brave Kinmont Willie cried.

" I'll up and away with you my men :
    Small thanks for their courtesie
Who lodged me in these goodly walls,
    With such winsome companie.

" I'll up and away, my trusty men,
    But the reckoning I will pay,
With compound interest on the debt,
    When we meet some other day."

They have reached the second door—'tis passed
    With a swift and stealthy stride ;
They hurry on till the fifth and last
    On its hinges swingeth wide.

With a ladder of rope the outlaws three
    O'er the castle postern sprang ;
And faster fell the drenching rain,
    And louder the tempest rang.

Away, and away, through the cold mirk night,
    Three leagues they have travelled o'er,
As the slumbering warder at his post
    Hears the prison clock strike four !

They sought him east, they sought him west,
　　They sought him on land and sea ;
But Kinmont Willie led them a dance
　　That they danced right ruefullie !

Two thousand marks of the red, red gold,
　　And a pardon free to all
Who help to bring the caitiff back
　　To Carlisle's castle wall.

In vain they threaten, in vain they bribe—
　　Who cares for their worthless gold—
There's never a prison in Cumberland
　　Could Kinmont Willie hold !

They may seek him east, they may seek him west,
　　But Willie sailed over the sea ;
He'll pay them back with interest *yet*
　　For their goodly courtesie !

www.ingramcontent.com/pod-product-compliance
Lightning Source LLC
Chambersburg PA
CBHW022341020726
47500CB00004B/1231